Oops
Pounce
Quick
Run!

AN ALPHABET CAPER

To my mom

ISBN 978-1-338-25323-8

12 11 10 9 8 7 6 5 4 3 2 1   17 18 19 20 21 22

Printed in the U.S.A.   40

First Scholastic printing, October 2017

The artist used India ink and felt-tip pens to create the illustrations for this book.
Typography by Dana Fritts

Mike Twohy

OOPS POUNCE QUICK RUN!

AN ALPHABET CAPER

SCHOLASTIC INC.

Asleep

Ball

Catch

Dog

Eye

Feet

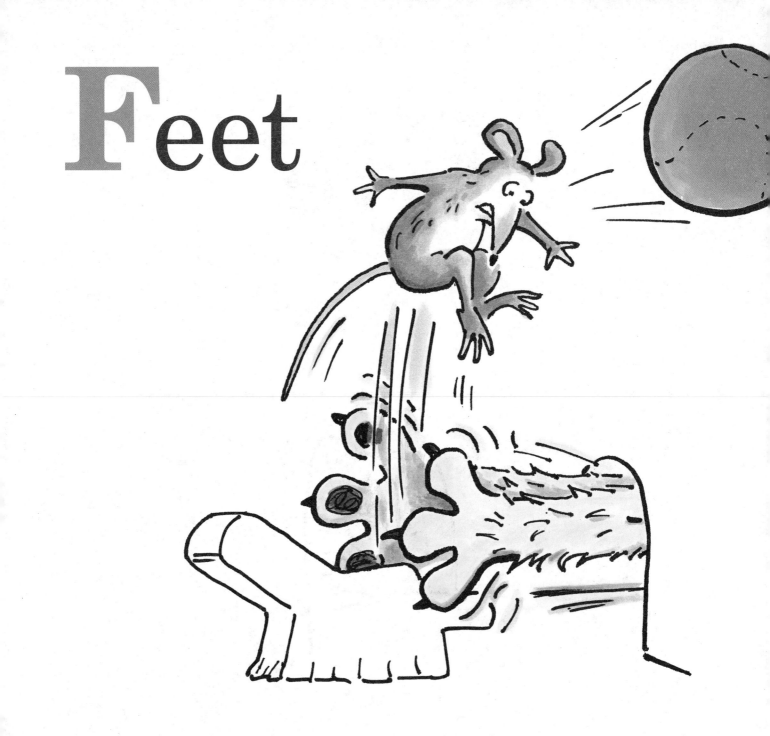

I'll chase!

Kitchen

Living room

Missing

Nowhere

Oops

Pounce

Quick!

Run

Safe

To Dog

Unwrap

Very cool

Wag

Xoxo

Yes!